Besties

Janae Marie

Copyright Page

Besties

Chapter 1
Wedding Bell Blues

Today, was one of the most amazing days of my life! Renewing my vows with my husband, Kevin Rose. I again, will be pronounced, Crystal Rose. My husband and I have shared many wonderful years together. See, we didn't have the finances all those years ago for a huge elaborate wedding. So, I just could not wait to walk down the aisle toward my king.

Sitting in the dressing room of the church while the bridesmaids fussed over my hair and makeup, I saw everyone except my maid of honor, Trish Yearwood. We'd been friends since childhood. She was my ride or die. We did everything together, even college.

I now work as an anchor for a prestigious news channel and Trish works as a reporter. Lost in my mental trance, a friend tapped me on the shoulder.

"How does it look, Crystal?" my bridesmaid, Amanda questioned.

"It looks great! You always do great work when I need it."

"Okay, where is everybody? Where is Trish? Anyway, let's go. It's time!"

"Oh, no! I'm not ready!" I squealed.

"Too late!"

I grabbed my bouquet and Amanda placed my veil over my face. We walked toward the chapel. Instantly, I felt butterflies in my stomach. Meanwhile, the pastor ran toward me in a panicked gate.

"Sister Rose, we have a slight problem. We haven't been able to find Brother Rose, nor Sister Yearwood."

Oh no! I thought.

I stormed into the chapel and searched around everywhere for my husband. I know he would show up. We'd planned our vow renewal ceremony over the past year. I looked all around and still couldn't find either one of them. I didn't know what was going on.

My friends approached me saying they'd finally found them both. I followed my bridesmaids and walked toward where they were leading me. I was sure I'd be letting my husband know that it is time to get the ceremony started. But instead, I get the biggest shock of my life.

The doors flew open of the storage closet, where I was told they were. My so-called husband was screwing my best friend against the wall of a freaking church in a closet. Everyone was appalled at this sight. I was truly disgusted.

They were going at it until I walked up to them. All his groomsmen and my bridesmaids were standing around.

They gathered themselves together and my husband just stared at me.

I walked right up to him and slapped the piss out of him. I was in a church, so I refused to curse. Trish walked right out of the room and began down the hall. I walked up to her and grabbed her arm.

"How the heck could you do this to me? This is my husband! What is wrong with you, Trish?"

"What?"

"What do you mean, 'what'? You just screwed my husband! My husband. You can't get your own man!"

"Your man? You're so silly. You mean, 'our' man. You remember when I told you I was pregnant? Guess, who the father is!" she said, rubbing her small belly.

"I've been trying to ruin your life since college. It's just now that you're finally catching on," she taunted.

I knew I was in the house of the Lord, but I just couldn't take it anymore.

"You bitch!"

I jumped on Trish and we began fighting. Yes, we were scrapping inside of a church. Everyone rushed over to us to break us up. I remember Amanda pulling me off Trish, attempting to hold me back. Full of adrenaline, I wanted to kick her ass as well as my husband's ass.

I saw him standing against the wall. He looked pathetic. I pulled my ring off my finger and threw it at him.

"It's over! Give me a divorce. Go be with that ho!" I yelled before me and my bridesmaids walked out of the chapel.

I knew Trish was a snake, but I tried to deny it. I tried to overlook it for many years. Seeing the things she did with other friends and even her sister. I just never thought she'd be the one to stab me in the back. It was plain to see that this bitch had it out for me. Sadly enough, this wasn't even the worse thing she'd done to me.

Chapter 2
Best Friends!

I remember our days at Spelman just like it was yesterday. Amanda, Trish and I were at the hottest party of the semester. There were cuties all over from the football and the basketball team. Let's not forget the Qs and the Kappa's. That is how I first met Kevin. Little did I know, he'd be a snake too.

Trish was the life of the party. Guys everywhere would flock to her. I was more reserved and laid back but I didn't let that stop me from having a good time. We were all scoping the room for a guy. I spotted a guy from the basketball team coming over to where I was standing.

"Hello, Ms. Lady. How are you?" The basketball player questioned. He had the prettiest eyes I'd ever seen. Of course, this was way before I met Kevin.

"I'm great. Thanks for asking," I answered shyly.

"I'm Rahul. What's your name beautiful?" he asked, with the most perfect smile I'd ever seen.

This guy was very easy on the eyes, tall caramel complexion with brown eyes…I was in heaven.

As we engaged in conversation, here come Trish with her flamboyant self.

"Hey, Girl!" she shouted, obviously drunk.

"Hey, Rahul, this is my friend and roommate, Trish."

"Nice to meet you, uh…Trish."

I'd been drinking so much punch, my bladder was about to explode. I excused myself and ran straight to the bathroom. When I returned to the party, I noticed no familiar faces. I searched top to bottom for Trish and Rahul and couldn't find them anywhere. I decided to find Amanda. She'd been dancing with a guy from her chemistry class. I whispered to her that I couldn't find Trish. I didn't care about finding Rahul anymore because I knew jocks were big time sluts around campus anyway. I was sure he wandered off with another girl. It was getting late and I had an 8 am class. The time was a quarter past one and people were slowly beginning to dissipate while Amanda and I were still at the party. We couldn't leave because Trish drove us there. She was our fucking ride. *Where the hell is our damn roommate?*

"Try calling her cell phone!" Amanda said in a panicked tone.

"I'll try." I called her phone, but it went straight to voicemail. "Um, Amanda…. She's not answering."

"What the hell do you mean she's not answering? You mean she just left us here?"

"Looks like!"

"That bitch! I can't believe she left us on the other side of town and didn't even tell us. How could she do this? How are we going to get back to school?" Amanda asked.

"How much money do you have? We're going to have to get an Uber or something."

Amanda was furious! I don't blame her. She left us, she left us at a party all by ourselves. She left without telling us. See, I don't know why I didn't realize how self-centered Trish really was. Guess, I was blind.

Me and Amanda pulled together our cash and ordered an Uber to get back on campus.

We made it back in twenty minutes and thankful to be safe. As we reached our dorm room, Amanda planned on cursing Trish out for leaving us. Once we stepped in, I saw Rahul coming out of her room buckling his belt while Trish is standing there in some lingerie.

I stood there in total disbelief. She'd left us for a dude! I didn't know whether to be pissed at this bitch for leaving us at the party or because she slept with the guy I was trying to get with. I'd tried so hard to hold on to our friendship over the years. That I look back and wonder why I'd ever befriended her in the first place.

"Oh, hey. What's up, Crystal?" Rahul asked as he left our room.

"How could you leave us at the party? We were there all alone with no ride to get home. We had to pay for an Uber! You need to fork up the cash and pay us back." Amanda yelled.

"So, what's the big deal? Y'all got home didn't y'all. No one said I had to take y'all home. Just because we arrive together; don't mean we have to leave together," Trish spat out with attitude.

"You little bitch! Anything could have happened to us. You don't even care about your roommates."

"Look, Amanda you need to chill."

"No, you need to chill before, I whip your ass."

"How could you sleep with Rahul? You saw me talking to him?" I interjected.

"So, it wasn't like that was your man or anything. All guys are up for grabs. Not my fault he liked me better. I won, you lost. Now if you don't mind, it's late. I'm about to get some sleep."

Trish walked away and closed her door. Amanda and I just looked at each other and disbelief. Shook our heads and turned in for the night.

Chapter 3
Nice-Nasty

The following after all the dust settled, we were sitting at the table eating breakfast with a few other students. Once again, Trish opened a can of worms. I tried to ignore her and take in the fresh smell of pancakes and bacon that filled the air of the dormitory cafeteria.

"You know, I'm really surprised on how good the food actually is. I was determined to not eat the food because I just knew dorm food would taste like prison food!" Amanda joked as she shoved a spoonful of grits into her mouth.

"Well, um, if you ask me, I think you need to watch what you eat." Trish stated.

Amanda stopped eating and looked dead at Trish.

"Excuse me! What did you just say?'

"Look, all I'm saying is just watch the calories. You're already a little on the plus side. Don't want you to blow up. Guys like thick chicks not fat chicks. I'm just saying."

I shook my head. I tried to ignore the obvious ignorant statement and continued to eat my hash browns.

"Who the hell do you think you are, calling me fat?"

"No, see, you're taking it the wrong way. I wasn't calling you—"

"You're damn right. First of all, my weight is not a problem for the guys that I date. I can keep a man unlike you, little Miss-I-sleep-with-everything-that-walks. Who the hell said you had to be a size zero to be sexy? If we weren't in this cafeteria; I swear I'd kick yo—"

"Girls like you are always making an excuse as to why you can't back away from the table. I bet date night for you is the drive through at Wendy's. Look all I'm saying is, it won't hurt you to hit the gym a few times a week. Might actually snag a man after you run a few miles on that treadmill."

That was it, Amanda totally lost it. She looked at me for a brief moment with a look of complete anger. Her pale Latina skin turned a bright red. Trish just rolled her eyes and continued drinking her cucumber water while Amanda threw her drink on her.

"Roommate or not. I will hurt you. You are a bitch who thinks she's so much better than everyone. I swear one day, you're going to get a wake- up call and it's not going to be pretty."

Trish threw something back at her and the ladies stepped away from the table and began fighting. The usual quiet cafeteria became an echo of roars. Fortunately, they stopped fighting before the Dorm Monitor came in.

Later

That

Day...

Back in the dorm, I saw Amanda coming through the door, still a little furious about what happened.

"Hey, you cool now?" I asked in concern.

"I can't take living with this chick. I'm going to kill her. I can't even get switched to another living space because all of the rooms in the dorms are booked to capacity until next semester. I'm going to be stuck with this chick until the spring semester is over!"

"You were going to move out?"

"Yes, look Crystal, you're my girl. But this chick has done enough damage to the both of us for me to know that she isn't a good person to be around. You can wait and hang around for hope that she'll become a better person, but I know better. Come on, she already left us at a party. Hell, what more signs do you need before you realize she's the common denominator to all our drama?"

I stopped typing on my MacBook Pro once I saw Trish walking in with shopping bags from Macy's, Victoria Secrets, Pink and Michael Kors. She walked toward her room. Amanda and I look at each other puzzled.

"Um, so you're not going to say anything?" I asked Trish.

"Say anything about what?" she replied, taking off her Prada sunglasses.

"About the crap you spewed earlier over breakfast. You didn't think it was hurtful?"

"I don't apologize. I meant what I said."

"Why'd you buy all that stuff? Did you pay for that stuff with your financial aid?" Amanda questioned.

"Um, no. This guy bought it for me! I would never spend my own money. Look at me! That's what I'm saying Amanda. If you looked like me, you'd get sugar daddies. Y'all better take note!"

"You're such a ho!" Amanda says.

"Stop hatin'. Dang, you're such a freaking hater. Get it together." Trish shot back.

"No, what you do in your own life is on you. But we've been asking you to buy—" I said trying to diffuse the situation.

"You can fuck for some clothes and shit. But you're hoe ass can't buy a five-dollar pack of tissue? Damn, we've been asking you to buy toiletries and cleaning supplies. But you always use our shit. Your sugar daddy couldn't buy your personal items. Stop asking me for tampons, when you get your period, if you're so much of a baddie! Can't stand this shit. I'm out!"

"You're such a liar! I'd never ask you for shit. Yes, please go! Stupid ass trick."

Amanda walked out of the room and Trish carried her bags to her room. I couldn't believe how rude and inconsiderate this girl was toward her. I know some girls just don't click, but dang, could this mess get any worse? I sat on the couch in the living room frustrated, upset and puzzled as to what to do with these girls.

Chapter 4
The Meeting

"I still can't believe that you are in a sorority. Wow, how does it feel? How are the guys? I know they look good." Amanda questioned excitedly.

It had been roughly six months since I'd crossed and became a full fledge Delta Sigma Theta. Yes, crimson and cream. I loved being a Delta. The opportunities given to us were unsurmountable. We did a lot of charitable work for the community. Although, what I loved the most were the step shows and of course, the parties.

One night, I was in my room getting ready for a party. Wearing my letters made me feel so proud. Plus, the benefit of meeting fine ass Kappa men was definitely number one on my priority list.

"It's great. I love it. Everybody knows I'm a member of the Crimson and Cream. By the way, are you coming to the party?"

"Can I come?"

"Of course. Just got to arrive there before 11pm to get in for free." I said as we were styling our hair in the bathroom mirror. Then in walked Trish, adding her two cents.

"I don't know why anyone needs to be a part of an organization to feel like you belong. Me on the other hand, I'm a team all by myself."

"Trish, do you have to share your opinion about everything? I mean if you want to go with us, you can?"

"Whatever. I'll have to see what else I have planned."

"I guess. Well, the party ends at 2 pm. Hopefully, you'll come. Me and Crystal are about to head out."

Later that evening at the party, I was super excited. Lemert Hall was packed. This was the party of the year. The music was popping with sounds of Cardi B, Nicki Minaj and Kendrick Lamar. The guys were looking good. I wasted no time getting my butt on the floor before the Deltas did their stride. I even spotted Amanda talking to a guy.

As I was dancing, a fine ass guy approached me. Obviously, a Kappa Alpha Psi. He was tall, brown skin and I couldn't take my eyes off of him.

"Hello, Miss Lady. What is your name?"
"My name is Crystal. What's yours?"

"Kevin. How long you been a Delta?"

"Six months."

"Oh okay, so you just crossed over. That's what's up. So, I'm going to see a lot of you around here then. You got a man? Are you seeing anybody?"

"Not at the moment. Nope."

"Well, you're seeing me now!"

I laughed at his lame attempt to ask me out. I had to admit. I was hooked. His Polo Blue cologne engulfed my senses. Couldn't help but be weak for him as he flashed his sexy ass smile.

We danced for hours and exchanged numbers before the party ended. Definitely, would be keeping in touch with him.

Two

Weeks

Later...

Things between Kevin and I were looking good. We were slowly becoming the most popular couple on campus. Everywhere you saw Kevin, you saw me and vice versa. But this would be the first time I'd bring him back to my room.

As we walked in, I saw my roommates sitting in the living room watching TV and reading a magazine. Instantly, Trish locked eyes with us.

"Crystal, who is this fine young man?" she asked, trying to play it off like she'd never seen Kevin before.

"Uh, Trish, Amanda, this is Kevin. Kevin these are my roommates."

"Nice to meet y'all. How y'all doing?"

"We good. Nice to meet you. You got any single frat brothers to introduce me to?" Amanda joked.

Kevin nodded his head in agreement and smiled. Trish walked over to Kevin and gave him a hug and kissed him on the cheek. Immediately, I shot her a stern look.

"Trish, Trish, what are you doing? Chill. You don't have to be so friendly. Come on, let's go Kevin. We can study in my room."

We started studying his psychology notes for a test he had on Thursday at Morehouse University. But who were we kidding. We both knew we had no plan on actually studying. Hmm, maybe studying some anatomy!

Chapter 5
When Temptation Hits / Kevin Rose

I received a call from my baby, Crystal, saying she was running late from her soror meeting and to meet her at her dorm. I stood outside the door until she came back but her roommate Trish happened to have arrived first.

"Hey! Kevin, right?"

"Yeah, I'm waiting on Crystal. Should be back any minute hopefully."

"Oh okay, well, I can let you in and you can wait in here until she comes back."

"Cool, thanks."

I followed this girl inside, but I had a funny feeling about her. I think she had a thing for me. She sat next to me on the couch as she turned on a movie and began bombarding me with questions. Trish was a little fine redbone. But I already had my brown skin cutie.

"So, Kevin, are you from Atlanta?"

"Um…yeah, born and raised. What about you?" I asked just to make conversation.

"Yeah, of course. You know you're really handsome. Crystal is really lucky to have someone like you. She doesn't always appreciate what she has. It would be such a shame for her to hurt a good man like you."

I could tell she was trying to come on to me. Everything inside of me was screaming for me to fight this urge; but she ran her hand up and down my leg. She kissed me, this time on the lips.

I didn't stop her at all. Luckily, it was just a kiss. Trish broke away from the kiss and smiled, grabbed her books and walked into her room. A few moments later Crystal walked in with the hugest grin on her face. I couldn't believe I'd just kissed my girl's roommate. There was no way I would tell her what happened. As long Trish and I never went any further than this.

"Hey, Baby," she said greeting me with a hug and a kiss.

"Hey Crys. How was the meeting?"

"It was great. Got a community event for next Saturday. Do you want to go grab something to eat? I'm starving?"

"Oh yeah, let's go!" I wanted more than anything to get the hell out that room with Trish.

****

The next week, I couldn't get Trish out of my head. Don't get me wrong, I loved Crystal. But she was always busy with school, work, internships and soror duties. We barely saw each other except for when we both had step shows or some kind of frat or soror meeting. Now Trish, her little freaky ass was always around. Easy access, that's it only. I stopped by the room while Crystal was in class.

Trish opened the door looking pretty good. We knew we didn't have much time; so, we got right to it. She led me to her bedroom and took lead.

Trish began to take my clothes off and kissed all over my chest. It felt so good, I knew it wasn't right. But then she pulled out my dick and placed it in her mouth. I hadn't received a good blow job in a hell of a long time because this was something Crystal refused to do. I would pick the one girl in Spelman with standards and morals. She was wife material. I knew I'd marry her someday. Meanwhile, Trish, she was the biggest slut on campus. Every man on Morehouse campus knew this shit. Before, I bust my nut I picked her up and threw her on the bed. As I began sexing Trish, she moaned and screamed my name. I wrapped my hand around her neck in an effort to mute her noises. Watching Trish squirm around the bed as I hit her just a little bit harder, help me finally bust my nut. Quickly, I placed my clothes back on before Crystal would ever have a chance to walk through the door. The last damn thing I needed was to get caught with this trick. I loved Crystal and I didn't want to lose her. Yeah, I knew it was wrong. I never thought it would go any further than this.

Chapter 6
Trish's Pain

"Yes! I got it! I can't believe it! I got it Amanda!" I heard Crystal squeal as I walked out of my bedroom and saw my two roommates talking in the living room.

What was this bitch talking about now? I thought. I rolled my eyes at her. She is always so damn happy. I bet she wouldn't be so happy if she knew I was screwing her man. Ooh, he was so good in bed. I most certainly, have to see him again.

"You got what? Should I be happy you got it. Or you got it like you need to medical help?" Amanda joked.

"No! Amanda! I got the internship. I'm going to be a news intern at FOX5 Atlanta! You just wait and see I'm going to be on TV soon!" Crystal bragged.

"Ah! Congratulations girl! I'm so proud of you! You're just killing it all around. Get it girl! Pretty soon, I'll be able to say, that's my friend on TV. We got to celebrate. Have you told Kevin yet?"

"No, I literally just read the email. I'm about to call him now. Thanks. Oh, hey Trish. Did you hear the good news? I'm going to be an intern at WAGA FOX5."

"Yeah, I was literally standing five feet away from you guys. Congrats, I guess. How's your man doing?" I asked matter-of-factly.

I sucked my teeth and left the room. I honestly couldn't stand Crystal. All this bitch did was brag. Always bragging on her damn self. That shit made me sick to my stomach.

Look at me, I'm a Delta. Look at me, I have a new boyfriend. Look at me, I'm working for FOX news. That bitch thought she was perfect. Had the perfect life. *Why did she get to have everything? What about me?* I deserved nice things too and I was going to get those nice things she had through any means necessary.

I was on my way to see Kevin at Morehouse for another hook up. Having sex with Kevin made me realize how imperfect little miss Crystal's life really was. She thought she had the most amazing boyfriend; but little did she know, her man was my man too.

His roommate let me in as he was on his way out the door. I was happy to see Kevin. I could tell he was just getting off the phone with Crystal.

"Yeah, yeah, that's really good, Crystal! I'm so proud of you, Baby! We got to get together and celebrate. Besides, I got something to ask you. Something very important to ask you. I love you, Baby. I got to go but I'll definitely see you later and talk about this little get together we're going to have. Alright, bye."

I stood in his room looking irritated. *How dare he be on the phone talking to that bitch while I'm in his presence. I was the main bitch around here.*

"What's wrong Trish? Why do you look so damn mad?"

"Why are you still wasting your time with her? When are you going to leave her and commit to me?"

"You're joking right? Why would I do that? I'm a Kappa, she's a Delta. We've already been together for damn near a year."

"So, what about me? We've been messing around for six months now. You can't tell me that I don't mean shit to you, Kevin."

"You know what it is, Trish. Stop acting like that. You know what you mean to me. Trish, stop being sensitive. I love you too," he said kissing my forehead. I brushed him off.

Immediately I was ready to walk out of his dorm room, but he was so damn sexy. He walked over toward where I was standing and entered me from behind. Again, he gave me what I yearned for. Sex with him was out of this world, amazing. He told me Crystal wasn't really giving it up how I was which is why he loved being with me. I was sure the only reason why he stayed with Crystal was because he's too afraid to break her heart. He really wanted to be with me. I knew it. I knew he wanted me instead. We would have to come clean to Crystal soon. Knock that bitch off of her almighty pedestal. And looks like her little celebratory party would be just the right time to do it.

The

Next

Weekend...

I attended Crystals' little party at *The Commerce Club,* a nice gathering place for food, music and dancing. There were a couple of tables for her sorority friends and frat brothers. Then, in walks this chick holding hands with my man. I sat next to Amanda, who gave me a faux smile. Everybody went around celebrating her. It was just a job, goodness. *They're acting like this bitch walks on air or something.*

Then, here comes Kevin, wanting to make an announcement. I wished he'd cut the crap and come clean with Crystal that he was leaving her to be with me.

"Hey, everybody! I want to say thank you for coming out and helping me and my girl celebrate a special night. I also want to say thank you to all my Kappa brothers. Y'all really been there for me. Also, to the Sorors who helped make this night possible. And to the most special woman in my world; Crystal Hall. Ever since I met you, my world has really felt complete. I have never meant anyone as special as you. I have something to ask you."

"What is it? This is kind of much just to celebrate a new job, Kevin."

I can't fucking believe it. I can't fucking believe what this man is doing right now. Is he... Oh no, he can't be? Don't tell me...He is...

"Will you, Crystal Marie Hall, marry me?" he asked, down on one knee.

This was unbelievable. He was supposed to be with me. That was my man. The cheers grew loud as Crystal accepted his proposal and he slid an engagement ring on her finger. Her finger! Again, this bitch kept winning. I couldn't believe she was getting married to him. I couldn't believe he loved her enough to want to marry her. Yet, he was sleeping with me. Nobody gave a damn about my feelings. Kevin said he wanted me. Hell, he told me he loved me. I couldn't understand why he was engaged to her. Why did Crystal get all the damn breaks in life while I received nothing in return. Her life was so easy. I wanted for once...just *once* for Crystal to get knocked off of her damn pedestal. Trust and believe; I was determined to make it happen.

Chapter 7
New Beginnings / Crystal

"You looked so great up there! All y'all looked good. How long does it take you guys to learn all those moves?" Amanda asked after I finished a set at the Black Greek Step-Show event at Morehouse.

"Thanks, Girl. We practiced for about two weeks. It was a lot of hard work. But it's been really fun. Doesn't Kevin look good up there?"

"Um, that's your fiancé so I don't feel comfortable speaking on him. Now Kevin did tell me he'd hook me up with that Steve though. He definitely looks good!"

"Okay, yeah I can see that. Steve has a 4.0 and he's a Pre-med student. Right up your alley, right?"

Amanda's facial expressions turned from shocked to elated. "Wow, Girl I still can't believe that you're engaged girl! How does it feel?"

"It's a good feeling. But I honestly just feel the exact same. I do though, enjoy looking at my ring!" I laughed.

"Congrats, Girl!" Another Delta stated walking past where I was standing.

"Thanks, Ashley!" I yelled back at her.

"So, are you ready for the honeymoon night?" Amanda questioned enthusiastically.

"Um, I guess! Ugh…yeah!"

"So, you guys haven't done anything yet?"

"We've messed around, but we haven't gone all the way yet. Got to give him something to look forward to. If I gave him everything right now, there wouldn't be a reason for him to marry me." I wholeheartedly believed and lived by that statement.

"I know you can't possibly believe that mess, can you?" Trish interjected as she cut into our conversation.

"Excuse me?"

"I mean seriously, you are dating Kevin Rose, a member of the Kappa Alpha Psi fraternity. There are girls throwing themselves at him all the time. I know you heard those girls screaming for them earlier. I mean, if he's not getting it from you, aren't you worried he'll get it from somewhere else?"

"First of all, I'm not that insecure. I'm confident in my relationship. Plus, if those girls are that easy to give it up to him, trust he'll never respect them. So, no I'm not worried. Because I know what I offer." I replied.

"You're so naïve," Trish stated rolling her eyes.

After, she made her foolish comment, Kevin came and kissed me on the lips in front of the entire crowd of fraternities', sororities and spectators as well. I was both excited and embarrassed. I've always been a private person. But I was glad that he was able to shut Trish up. That was my girl. But she was way too damn concerned about Kevin and I's relationship.

He grabbed my hand and we walked back to his room.

****

A week later, I was given an amazing opportunity at my internship. I had been there for a couple months and had the hang of things. One of the senior reporters entrusted me to write, report and produce a news story of my choice. I couldn't believe it. I got to report on a news story that would actually play live on the air. I was totally geeked at that point!

"We are live at the city council building where all of the city council members are discussing today's budget cuts to homeowners, and education. There are several people against the budget cut and they're certainly vocal about their opinions inside. This has been Crystal Hall, reporting for FOX 5 Atlanta. Back to you, Tina in the studio."

As soon as the camera guy gave me the cue that we were no longer live. I squealed loudly! I was so excited. Especially, after the senior reporter, said I did great. I practiced so many years in the mirror for that moment. I couldn't wait to become a reporter.

"Very good, Crystal. Just relax a little bit more. Remember, it's like you're talking to a friend. No need to be so tense. I know you were nervous but perhaps after you graduate, you can apply to be a reporter. I'll certainly put in a good word for you," Timothy Wells, the senior reporter advised.

"Oh, wow. Thank you so much, Tim. I appreciate this so much." I said, jumping up and down.

I had to call my parents and tell everyone. We packed up our equipment and headed back to the station. I had to edit my story and make it ready for broadcast at 5 pm. Right then, I was on cloud nine.

Graduation was less than a year away, I practically had a job lined up already. Plus, I was engaged to the love of my life. I couldn't wait to be Kevin's wife. Mrs. Crystal Rose. Yes, that had a wonderful ring to it. But not compared to the ring he put on my finger; that diamond cut ring looks so good! Of course, that wasn't the reason why I was marrying him. The ring was just icing on the cake.

****

Later that day back at the dorms, I ran into Amanda on our way back to our room.

"Hey, Girl! How you doing? You're coming back from your internship?"

"Yes, Girl! I got great news!"

"What is it? Oh wait, I have to tell you! I'm going out with Steve this weekend! Maybe you and Kevin can double date with us?"

"Oh, sure that's no problem. Look forward to it. I'm going to be on the news! They let me cover a story. It should air during the 5 pm broadcast."

"What? Really? What time is it? Oh crap, it's almost five now." She grabbed my arm and rushed into the room and turned on the TV. "Trish, we need to watch Crystal on the news."

"Why?" Trish asked annoyed.

"I got to report on a story," I said quietly.

"Oh shoot, there you go! You look great! You looked a little nervous though."

"Hell, I was! But the good thing is, the reporter said he'll try to put in a good word for me to be a reporter at the station after graduation."

"Dang, that's a sweet hookup."

"Wow, you did good Crystal," Trish complimented me.

"Congratulations. I know I haven't been the biggest supporter of you. But I really wanted to say congrats to you. I'm really glad that things are going so well for you and Kevin," she responded while giving me a hug and a smile.

"Um...thank you."

I didn't really know how to take Trish giving me a compliment because it didn't really seem genuine.

Maybe she really did mean it. I mean, people can change. I knew Trish a long time and I was sure she was just going through some personal things, so I never took what she did to heart. That was my best friend... Right...

Chapter 8
Black Mail this Black Male / Kevin

Being at Morehouse, made me feel like the big man around campus. Plus, everything in my life was going great. Crystal would soon be my lovely wife, the Kappas were doing great things in the community. A job would soon open up for me as an apprentice for an electrical engineer, five minutes away from campus. The money in my bank account was adding up. There wasn't anything that I regretted right now.

Making my way back to my dorm room, I was ready to hit the bed. It might have been the middle of the afternoon but I was exhausted, from classes, step practice, meetings. There was barely any time for me to get a nap in. Walking into my room, I got the biggest shock of my life. Trish standing in my bedroom.

"How the hell did you get into my room?" I questioned.

"Don't worry about that? I just want to know how the hell can you marry her instead of me? How the hell do you think I would accept that? You told me you loved me. Yet, you slipped a ring on her finger instead of mine."

This girl was bugging. Did she honestly think we had something going on besides sex? Why do girls who know a dude got a girl, think the guy will leave the girl for them? Duh, come on now.

"You know, Trish, I think we should just stop messing around. I'm engaged now. I really do love Crystal."

"What? We should stop messing around. All because you're engaged! Where was all that love when you had me bent over the desk. Where was all that love when you were coming to my room while she was in class? How much did you love her then, Kevin? Why do I get tossed to the damn side because you had a change of heart?"

"Trish! You knew what it was. I'm sorry if you feel like I hurt you. But you knew I had a girl."

"No! You knew you had girl too! It's not just on me! But you know what? If you stop seeing me, I'm going to tell Crystal everything we've been doing behind her back. I am sure you don't want your pretty little fiancé to find out the dirt that's been going on behind her back."

"Trish, don't play that guilt trip shit on me." I really didn't have any energy to play with this girl.

"I don't want to deal with you anymore, Trish. Let it go." I said pushing her towards the door to get her to leave my room.

"Kevin! I'm not playing with you. I will tell her everything. We're roommates, trust I will tell her. Tell her how you screwed me the day before you proposed to her. Don't play with me."

"So, you want me to keep screwing you because you mad, I didn't marry you. Girl, please. It'll be my word against yours. Who do you think she'll believe, me or you? Get the hell out of my room."

"Alright, Kevin. Don't believe me. But best believe, you don't want this secret to get out. Do you want to break Crystal's heart? Or do you want to hold on to your sweet little lie? I can help you have the best of best worlds. What man doesn't want two women? Crystal will never ever have to know?" she propositioned me as her fingertips softly touched my chin.

"I know you still want all this Kevin. Just make sure I'm happy and your girl will stay happy. Nobody gets hurts. Nobody suspects anything."

She kissed me softly on the lips, neck, chest and continued going south. I didn't want to deal with Trish anymore. But I was in too deep. I didn't want Trish to tell Crystal a damn thing. I loved Crystal. What was I supposed to do? Tell her, and risk losing the love of my life? Or keep seeing Trish and hope that she keeps her big ass mouth shut. Plus, I was getting my sexual needs met. Crystal made a vow to wait until we jumped the broom for us to go all the way. I admired that about her. She had morals, values, standards and principles. What guy wouldn't want that out of a woman? But right now, at this moment, my dick needed pussy. If Trish wanted to whore herself out, then hell that was her problem. As long as she kept her mouth shut. I didn't have a problem with it. It wouldn't last long anyway. Crystal and I would be married soon.

Six

Months

Later...

Chapter 9
Operation Sabotage / Trish

The time grew closer and closer for graduation. Time to get serious about plans for the future. I began interning at the same company Crystal was working at. Hell, she wasn't the only one that could tell the news. *Why should she get to be the only one on TV? She isn't even all that damn pretty.* I knew I looked better than her which was why her man was sleeping with me behind her back. He just doesn't want to lose her because he's obviously using her for money or something. Anyway, the look on her face as she saw me walk into the studio as I approached where she was standing was priceless.

"Hey, you're here early, that's great! Crystal, we have a new intern today, Trish Yearwood. I need you to show her around and get her accustomed to things around here." Jerry Smits, the News Director stated before he walked away.

"Oh, hey Girl. I didn't know you were interested in broadcast media?" Crystal questioned.

"Yeah, I think it's cool to be on TV."

"Um…it's a little more than just being on TV. It's a lot of hard work and research. But anyway, let me show you around. As you know this is the studio. This is what everybody at home gets to see. That there, is the anchor desk. This is where I plan to be in a few years! Over here are the cameras, computers and teleprompters. It's not that much. The hard work is done in the control room."

Crystal continued showing me around the studio thinking I really gave a damn about her little tour. I just had one plan and one plan only. Honestly, enough, I had to admit, the news station looked amazing. From the hazy blue lights hanging from the ceiling to the decorative arrangement around the room. I couldn't believe that she had the privilege of working here.

"Hey, we're about to air the news packages soon. I want to show you really quickly how I edited my story before it goes live on air. Okay, here is where we do the post-production. We edit the stories down to get them to fit in five to seven minutes."

She really wanted to help me. Crystal actually thought all this interested me. I envied her determined spirit.

"Wow, that's really interesting. Is this your story?"

"Yeah, it's ready to go live on the air. Just have to shoot it to the producer and it'll be broadcast to thousands of homes across the city." She said.

"Hey, Crystal, I need to speak to you about something!" Jerry, the News Director stopped in.

"Alright, I'll be right there. Uh, I have to go but you can finish checking out the equipment in the control room. I'll be right back." Crystal advised as she walked out of the room.

Now it was time for me to put my plan into action. I had the chance to open the files where Crystal's video footage was located. If this girl, thought she had something to show; not tonight. I took the entire video file and deleted it. Yup, I didn't care at all.

Later that evening during the live broadcast, I heard some people asking for Crystal's story. She began panicking when it just couldn't be found. Hearing her get yelled at by the producer, brought me some sick, twisted pleasure.

In a frustrated stance, I saw Crystal racing back toward the editing room.

"Hey, Trish, do you know what happened to my work? It was supposed to air at 5:15pm but the producer said he didn't have it. He said it wasn't on the drive. Now I have to find it."

"Oh, no! I don't know what happened to it. I don't even know how to work the video editing equipment." I lied.

"Uh, I can't believe this! This has never happened to me before." Crystal panicked.

I laughed silently to myself as I watched her try to recover the files from the news desk. I sat next to her at the workstation as she stared at the Mac computer, puzzled, praying for her work to be found.

"Where is your work, Crystal? It was supposed to be up and ready to go already. This has never happened before with you. What's going on?" The news director questioned her.

"I have no idea, Mr. Smits. I may have it on a backup disk, and I'll have it available for the 6 o'clock broadcast. I am so sorry, Mr. Smits."

"That's fine. Get it ready for the 6o'clock news. And make sure it never happens again!" He said in an aggravated but firm tone as he continued into the control room.

"I can't believe this has happened. I only have about twenty minutes for this to air. I wish I could help you out more. But it's really not a good time for me right now. Maybe next time."

"Oh no, I completely get it. No worries at all. I'm sorry, you couldn't find the video you put together. I hope you find it soon and everything gets straightened out. Unfortunately, it's time for me to take off."

"Oh, thanks so much! It's not your fault. I'm positive I have it saved to a drive somewhere." She said.

I shrugged my shoulders and turned away, leaving the station. Slowly, Crystal would be knocked off of her high-almighty pedestal. Secretly sabotaging her life and determined to win at any cost.

Two

Weeks

Later...

Chapter 10
The Wedding

It was an unusual evening. Kevin picked me up from work and told me that a huge surprise was awaiting me when we get home. I could only imagine what it could be. When we approached our home; he placed a blindfold over my eyes. Guiding me into the house, I felt butterflies fluttering all around my stomach. I couldn't wait for tomorrow. It would be our big day. Our wedding day.

"Come on Kevin! What are you doing?" I questioned.

"Be patient. Just a little bit longer," he said as we stepped into the house and removed the blindfold.

I opened my eyes and saw rose petals all over the living room leading toward the bedroom. My mouth dropped. It was the sweetest thing he'd ever done for me.

"I hope you like it. It's to celebrate your promotion to reporter at your job. Plus, you know we're getting married tomorrow. I just want to make it special for you. What do you think?"

"I love it! This is so romantic," I replied.

As I walked into the bedroom, there were twelve long stem roses laying on the bed. I couldn't help but start crying. This man was so amazingly sweet to me. There was no way I could wait to marry him.

He walked up to me and gave me a tight squeeze and kissed me passionately. Kevin touched all over my body. We fell down on the bed and he began to undress me. As his hands caressed my thighs, I felt him enter me. I let out some moans as he penetrated my vagina. Slow then fast, as the pace intensified with every beat of his stroke. I could tell he enjoyed hearing me whisper his name.

"I can't wait to marry you tomorrow," he whispered back to me. If this was what I had to look forward to after we were married, then I couldn't either.

The

Next

Day...

*T*oday is my wedding day. Today is my wedding day! Kevin and I didn't have the money for an elaborate wedding; so, we had a small ceremony at the courthouse. Our friends and family attended as witnesses and I couldn't have been any happier. Knowing that I would be spending the rest of my life with the love of my life brought a sense of overwhelming joy to my heart.

The judge entered the court and began the ceremony. Seeing Kevin standing in front of me was an amazing feeling. A few tears dropped from my eyes. I turned my head and saw everyone looking elated.

His vows were the most romantic I'd ever heard.

"To my best friend, lover and now my wife; the day has finally arrived where I get to spend the rest of my life with a beautiful, talented and amazing woman. You bring out the best of me and make me want to be a better man. I promise with all of my heart and soul that I will do my best to provide for you, take care of you. Honor and respect you, through thickness and through thin. Through sickness and through health. I love you Crystal Marie Hall and I promise to be the best husband and best friend, father to our future children to you."

"Oh, my gawd! I can't handle this!" I cried, as tears dripped from my eyes.

"I have never in my life met a man as sweet and amazing as you. You are my best friend, partner and confidant. I promise to love, cherish, honor and obey you. I love you with all of my heart and can't wait to spend the rest of my life with you. Thank you for being patient and honest with me always."

We say our 'I do's' and the judge declared the phrase, *I now pronounce you man and wife. You may now kiss your bride.*

Just like that we were married and I couldn't believe it. The cheers from the audience made everything seem so real. Once we left the courthouse, there was a photographer ready to take our photos. We walked to a scenic area to film our photos and videos and people in cars honked at us in celebration. This day couldn't have gotten any better.

After the wedding stuff was over, me and Kevin were on a plane to Costa Rica for our honeymoon. Since I received a preview of what was to come the night before, I was ready to get this started.

Two

Years

Later...

Chapter 11
Reality Sets In / Kevin

"I told you that I want to focus on my career first!" my wife yelled at me as we argued about starting a family for the third time in six months.

"Dammit, Crystal. We've been married for two years now. I told you that I wanted to settle down and start a family. You're still worried about your damn career," I mouthed off, pacing back and forth in our living room.

"Yes, my dreams of being a news anchor are almost here and I can't take a chance on getting pregnant right now because I'll have to go on maternity leave and then my chances will be gone."

"So, you care more about that damn job then you do your own damn husband?"

"No, Kevin. You know that it isn't true at all. Why are you acting like this? I just want to put it off for a while. Children are something that you shouldn't take lightly. Once I become an anchor, I'll have more money and—"

"Then what? Then it'll be some other damn goal for you to achieve. Next, you'll want to be a producer. Crystal, cut the crap, I've tried to be patient, but this is just ridiculous."

"Where are you going?" she questioned as I grabbed my keys and headed out the door.

I just couldn't deal with it anymore. What was so wrong with wanting to start a family with my wife? Hell, that's why people get married. Truth be told, Crystal worked so much, we barely had time for sex. I worked as an electrical engineer, but I came home every night to her. But she would have to go to bed early and be at work at 4 am. She would come home around 2 pm. I'd be at work. So, when we had the chance to see each other, we're too damn tired to do anything. Our first year of marriage, was wonderful but Crystal became complacent. She stopped making any effort to satisfy my needs.

I jumped in the car and headed to my favorite spot. I sat in the parking lot and dialed up a friend.

"Hey, what's up? Yeah, it's me. What are you doing right now? Yeah, can you meet me at the usual spot. Yup, the Marriott. Okay, I'm here already. I'll check in and put your name on the list. Just let me know when your downstairs. Alright, see you soon!"

I know what you're thinking. This is wrong. Hey, maybe it is but what can I do? I grew tired of Crystal not being available for me.

I checked into the hotel and told the clerk I had a plus one arriving shortly. Quickly, showered and squirted on some Issy Misaki cologne and awaited a text from Trish. I continued seeing Trish off and on behind Crystal's back. We were discreet. We made sure that Crystal would never find out about us. My phone buzzed and I knew she was waiting downstairs. I told her to come on upstairs to the room.

A soft knock came at the door and I couldn't wait to open it and see Trish.

Never once did she disappoint me. This girl took off her coat and revealed a pink and black lingerie piece. She closed the door and immediately we got down to business.

Trish took the reigns as she pushed me down on the bed. She pulled my dick out from my boxers and placed it inside her pussy. Trish began riding me like a horse. I placed my hands around her fat ass and enjoyed her bouncing on my dick. Sex, mind blowing sex is what I missed from my marriage. Sex with Trish was regrettably, better than with Crystal. Trish was a ho and Crystal a bit too reserved. She didn't want to relax and get wild. Meanwhile, Trish planted soft gentle kisses on my chest and continued downwards as she reached my dick and then gave me a blowjob. I could feel myself about to nut as my penis began to pulsate. I turned her around and entered her from the back. Trish started yelling and screaming. It just made me hit her harder. I tried to pull out, but she felt so damn good. I felt myself about to cum but didn't catch myself in enough time. *Fuck, I came inside Trish. Hope she don't get pregnant. What have I done? I certainly don't want a baby with this bitch.*

Chapter 12
You Can't Hide From Me Now! / Trish

Kevin and I went too far this time. I'd just came back from the doctor's office. I'm pregnant. I am now carrying Crystal's husband's baby. As excited as I was to be having a baby with her man. I didn't know how Kevin would take the news of him fathering my baby. The calls and text went unanswered as I tried to reach him. It'd been almost three weeks. It became clear that he didn't want to talk to me. Tired of sitting around for him to get back with me, I drove down to his job at Neel & Schaefer.

The receptionist buzzed me in as the building was heavily secured. As I approached the security desk of where she was sitting, she politely asked me what my visit was in regard to.

"Oh, I'm here to see my husband, Kevin Rose. I need to talk with him."

"Okay, just a moment as I get a hold of his department. You can have a seat while you wait."

About fifteen minutes later, I heard a voice that sounded a lot like Kevin.

"My wife is here to see me. Are you sure? This is usually the time she is at work at the station."

"Yes, Sir. I'm sure, she's waiting in the lobby for you."

As Kevin walked through the lobby, he looked confused. I called out to him and he came running over.

"Nice to see you here."

"Trish, what the hell are you doing here? Why are you telling people at my job that you are my wife? You crazy or something?"

"Because I'm tired of you avoiding me. I'm pregnant and you aren't talking to me."

"Trish, I don't even know if this is my baby. Besides, even if you are pregnant with my baby. I'm not leaving my wife for you. You knew the risk of sleeping with a man who is already involved. What the hell do you want from me? I don't give a damn about you or that damn baby."

I couldn't believe Kevin was being so cold hearted.

"Now if you'll excuse me, I have to get back to work and if you ever come back to my job again, I will have you arrested," he said before walking away.

"Kevin! Kevin! You have to talk to me." I tried to get him to reason with me. But he just continued walking away.

Stuck. What the hell would I do with a baby all by myself? I had to get Kevin to see that he needed to be with me. Besides, he told me Crystal wouldn't give him a family anyway. So, he had one with me. All we needed to do was get her out of the way and we'd be the perfect family. I just needed to get him to realize that.

I left his job and returned back to my apartment. Determined to get him to realize what he'd done, I began calling his phone and leaving voicemail messages. Angry ones. *How dare this man try to ignore me?*

Every afternoon, I parked across from his job and followed him home and sent threatening emails. I did whatever I could to get his attention. I was not going to be raising this baby alone, even if it took breaking up his alleged happy home.

Chapter 13

Sneaking Around: Crystal

For some odd reason, today felt quite unusual. I'd gotten use to Trish working along with me at the news station. She worked herself up from intern to reporter status. I heard rumors that she slept with our news director to get the job but since I didn't like to believe in rumors, I didn't know how true it was. When I saw her walking around the office, she looked a tad bit differently.

"Hey, Trish, when did this happen?" I said pointing towards her protruding belly.

"Ah, this! Um, about six months ago!"

"Oh wow! That's great! Congratulations! Who's the father?"

I had never seen Trish with any one so seeing her with a baby certainly surprised me.

"I've been seeing this guy, Justin. Yeah, he's a great guy. Who knows, maybe we'll get married soon, like you and Kevin."

"Yeah, I would love to meet this Justin. Why don't we have a dinner party at my house? It can be like a little double date thing."

"Sure, that sounds awesome!"

"Okay, let's make it Saturday around 4pm."

"We'll be there."

I shot Trish a smile and walked over towards my desk. It was certainly nice to see Trish about to have a child. It was a gift I wanted to give to Kevin. Since I'd recently been promoted to reporter I'd worked harder to snag an anchor position to secure our financial future before we brought children into the world. Kevin and I hardly spent any time together at that point.

As I prepared dinner, I saw Kevin coming home from another day of work. I couldn't wait to tell him about the party. He threw his bag on the couch and walked into the kitchen.

"Hey, Crystal. How was work?"

"Hey, Babe! Same ol' same ol'. But the stories are always crazier than the last. How was it for you?" I questioned giving him a kiss on the cheek.

"It's work. Ain't much to talk about. What's for dinner?"

"Your favorite, baked chicken and macaroni and cheese. Oh, I have good news. I'm having a party this Saturday. You know, me, you, Amanda, Steve, Trish and her new beau."

"Trish! Why are you inviting her over?"

"Because she is prego and has a new boyfriend that I'd love to meet. We're friends. I just want to meet her new…"

"You should've asked me before you just decided to invite people over. What were you thinking? Is that why you're cooking my favorite meal because you thought I'd be okay with it? Come on Crystal, I'm your husband. You need to think before you do shit like this. Communicate, damn!" he mouthed off walking out of the kitchen.

I didn't even have a chance to get a word in edgewise before he left to go upstairs. Kevin's attitude made me wonder why he was so against this dinner party. It made me want to have this party even more to find out the answer.

Later that evening, after I finished cooking, he came back down to eat dinner with me. We barely spoke a word as we watched the news and an old episode of *Living Single* on TV.

The day of the dinner party finally came and so far, everything appeared to be going great. Amanda and I were chatting and finishing up meals. Kevin and Steve were in the den watching a football game. Suddenly, the doorbell rang and I ran to answer it. As I opened the door, I saw Trish standing on my doorstep with a rather tall, brown skin guy with hazel eyes and a wide smile.

"Come in, come in! Oh, is this Justin?" I asked.

"Sure is."

"Congrats on the baby!" I said to them. Trish smiled while Justin looked albeit puzzled.

"Oh, he's shy. We don't really get a chance to get out much. This is like our first time out since we found out about the baby," she said.

"Well, the guys are in the den while Amanda and I are just about done with the food. Just take a seat and we'll be getting started shortly."

Before I could finish talking to Trish, Amanda pulled me into the kitchen.

"Yes, Amanda, what is it?"

"Why did you invite her?"

"Because she's our friend. You sound like Kevin. Why wouldn't I invite her?"

"Come on, Girl. She's pregnant and we've never seen her with a guy?"

"Amanda you're tripping! You know how she use to be in college. Hell, she's taken a couple of guys from me before."

"Be sure she still isn't taking a few from you now."

"Amanda, I'm married now."

"Yeah, I know and if you want it to stay that way, keep her the hell away from your man. I sure as hell know that I will," Amanda stated.

I rolled my eyes and began to bring the food to the table. The guys made their way towards the table and sat down. Everyone sat and began eating.

Kevin got up to grab another pitcher of ice water while Trish offered to help bring the last two pitchers out as everyone else remained seated and got acquainted.

"So, who is this Justin dude?"

"He's my brother, Kevin. Besides, why do you care who the hell he is? How long are we going to keep this charade up for your wife? I have to pretend I'm her damn friend and that I'm dating my own brother just to keep your secret going."

"Look, I'm simply trying to keep my marriage together. I don't want shit to do with you or the baby. I told you this already."

"Oh, Kevin, please. When are you going to stop lying to yourself? You know it yourself that you still want me. That's the problem. You are just like every other man. Want their cake and eat it too." Trish said as she caressed Kevin's stomach and touched his face slightly. Before she could kiss him, Steve walked in to see what was taking them so long.

"Um, hey. Y'all alright in here?"

"Yeah, let me get these water pitchers out to the table." Trish said as she walked back to join the party.

"Hey, what's going on here?"

"Nothing, Man. Nothing."

"It looks like you're messing around on Crystal. I hope that I'm wrong. Crystal's a good girl; she loves you, Homie. Don't do that to her," Steve advised.

"Too late, you know that baby she's carrying. It's mine."

"Awe Man, come on, Kevin. Tell me you playing? Tell me you're playing. How could you do that to her?"

"Shit, just sort of happened."

"Naw, shit like that doesn't just "happen". "

"Can you keep it a secret please?"

"Fine. But you're wrong man. Crystal deserves better than this, Man,"

Steve walked back to the party and Kevin stood in the kitchen thinking about what was said.

After the party ended and all of the guests departed, something didn't quite feel right as I cleared the table with Kevin. I just had to get to the bottom of what was aching at my gut.

"Kevin, can I ask you a question?"

"Sure, what is it? The dinner party went pretty well don't you think?"

"Yeah, it did. But there's just one thing that is eating at me. Be honest with me. Is there anything going on with you and Trish? You two seemed to take an awful long time to get two pitchers of ice water that were chilling in the refrigerator."

"Are you accusing me of sleeping with this woman? Why are you being so damn insecure? How long have we been married? Now, you want to pull this shit. Unbelievable!"

"Kevin Lamont Rose! Don't you dare pull that shit with me? If you waited until we got married to start messing around on me, I swear I will divorce your ass in a heartbeat," I threatened him.

"You know, Crystal. I love you. I would never cheat on you. But the fact that you don't even trust your man, is beyond me. Maybe you should check yourself. Stop listening to your single friends. Why would you accuse me of something like this? Maybe if you wouldn't work so much, you wouldn't feel so insecure in our marriage. Stop putting the blame on me when it's you that needs to take a look in the mirror. Are you doing your job as a wife to keep me happy?"

He walked off toward the den to watch another game of football. I couldn't believe what Kevin said to me. I loved Kevin with all my heart. I have played naïve when I had to. I have played weak when he needed, and strong when the situation arose but if this man were cheating on me, I honestly didn't know how I would take it. Almost five - years of marriage and I was determined to make it work.

Chapter 14
No Baby on Board / Kevin

"Where are you going? Can't we talk about this?" my wife cried out to me.

"Let me go! I just want to go out for a few drinks. I just need a break. Goodness. I'm tired of going over the same things over and over with you. I told you what I wanted. How many times can we have this discussion? Now I'm going out for a drink. I just want some time to myself. Stop smothering me." I said snatching her hand away as she tried to hug me. Rejecting her embrace, I threw her a look of disgust, grabbed my keys and headed out the door.

Driving, all I could think of was how frustrated I'd became in our marriage. Perhaps, it was the idea of not having the family as of yet with Crystal that I longed for. But then again, maybe it was the overwhelming guilt coming over me for cheating and having a child outside of my marriage. How could I look Crystal in the eye when I knew I hadn't honored the commitment towards our vows?

I had to tell her. Who was I kidding. Hell no. I couldn't do that. I pulled up to Lucky's Lounge and decided to drink the guilt away. The faint smell of cigars and a bit of marijuana filled the air as people played pool, watched sports and ate appetizers. I took a seat at the bar as the bartender asked for my drink order. My phone buzzed in my pocket as I took sips of my Cîroc.

Someone patted me on the shoulder, startling me. Turning around I saw my buddy Steve, smiling.

"Hey Boy, how are you doing?" he asked, giving me some play.

"I'm good. Just had to get some relaxation in. You know, do some thinking."

"Yeah, you talked to Crystal about what's going on yet?"

"Naw, Man. We got into a huge fight. I can't talk to her. Just being around her is too much for me to bear. Hard to look a woman in the eyes when…"

"You know you're living a lie. Man, maybe if you confess to her what is going on, she'll understand."

"Are you crazy? How am I going to tell my wife that I've been sleeping with her best friend from college and we're having a child together? I don't think she'll take that lightly. One word comes to mind when I think of what's going on. Divorce. I love Crystal. But I messed up. I messed up big time. This shit eating at me, Man. I thought

I'd be able to handle it but when Trish got pregnant, the shit about to hit the fan."

"You got two choices. Either you're going to confess to Crystal, and you two split up, or you keep it to yourself and act like the two of you are the happiest married couple in the world! Whatever decision you choose, think about how it will affect Crystal not just you."

"I hear you, Man. I hear you."

Listening to Steve's advice really made me realize how much I truly loved Crystal and couldn't believe that now I was risking losing her over a woman I didn't even want a future with. What the hell was I thinking. We caught the end of a basketball game before the bar closed for the night and the time came for me to drive home.

Honestly, the truth is something I should have shared with my wife, but I just couldn't hurt her anymore. I had to keep this a secret for as long as I possibly could. I could not risk this blowing up in my face. But knowing how vindictive Trish was, I was sure it would happen sooner or later.

I made it home and I placed the keys on the nightstand by the door. Making way through the living room, Crystal shot me an angry stare.

"Where the hell were you all night? Do you know what time it is? I was worried sick about you! I called you. I texted you. You ignored me. I am your wife. But I'll be damned if I'm going to keep putting up with your blatant disrespect. What the hell is wrong with you anyway?"

"You're right, and I apologize. I haven't been myself lately. For that—"

"I have been stressing myself out trying to be the best wife to you. I have been trying to give you everything that you wanted. Even a family! You have been such an ass. I wanted to tell you that I went to the doctor a little while ago and I found out about this."

My wife slid me a white folded up piece a paper. To my surprise, my wife had been pregnant for two months now and didn't know it. All that time I'd yelled at her for not giving me a family and there she was giving me everything I ever wanted.

"I'm so sorry. This is great news," I said as I walked over to give Crystal a hug.

"Don't hug me. Don't get too excited. Because um…I lost it two weeks ago."

"What do you mean that you lost it?"

"I miscarried, Kevin! Damn, all this time I needed you to be here for me. But all you were doing was stressing me out. Between that and work, that's how I lost the baby. I wanted to come to you and tell you that yes Kevin we will have the family that you wanted. I will place my desires and career plans on hold for you because that's how much I love you. But when you didn't think that you were getting what you wanted from me, you didn't even give me a chance to talk things through. You just yelled at me. Walked out on me like I didn't even matter to you. I'm sorry Kevin. I tried. I tried to give you what you wanted. I tried to give you a family. I didn't mean to lose the baby."

Crystal cried tears of sorrow, pain and regret. I felt nothing but sympathy and remorse. I could have kicked myself knowing I caused this much pain to my wife. Losing a baby is one of the worst feelings in the world. There was no way I could make this right. But I wanted desperately to make this up to her. Somehow, someway…

"All I can say is, I'm so sorry, Crystal. I'm so sorry." I hugged my grieving wife and let out some tears of sorrow myself. I held my wife all night, comforting her. Hopefully, taking away the pain that I caused within her heart.

Chapter 15
Let's Get Away!

Breaking the news to my husband that I'd lost our baby completely devastated me. The hardest thing I ever had to do in my life. The emotions that I felt were painful. I felt like I let him down. I felt like I let myself down. I cried every day. Kevin was the only one I told about the miscarriage. I barely held it together at work. But I knew eventually I had to put the loss behind me. How can you get over losing a child. You can't. There will always be that aching feeling of loss and regret plaguing the back of your mind.

Pulling up to the home felt different this time, now that the cat was out of the bag and Kevin knew the truth. I knew we could try again but this just wasn't a good time. He greeted me at the door with a bouquet of flowers and two plane tickets.

"What's all this?"

"I just want to prove to you that I am here for you. You've been through a lot and it's time we get away from reality for a while. That's why I booked us a first-class ticket to Costa Rica. You know where we went on our honeymoon. Kind of want to make it up to you."

"That's so sweet Kevin. I can't believe it. When do we leave?"

"In two hours!"

"Kevin. I haven't even packed. What about work? I can't leave right now..."

"Crystal. I took care of all that. I packed our bags and talked to your boss down at the station. He said, you had plenty of vacation time to use anyway. So, let's go baby. Grab your passport and let's fly to Costa Rica. You know we need this trip!"

I had to admit this was the Kevin that I truly loved and knew. He was so sweet and compassionate. This man was my best friend. We grabbed our bags and headed toward the airport. Couldn't wait to get to Costa Rica and bring back our honeymoon memories.

We stepped on the plane all smiles knowing we were headed to paradise.

A Few

Days

Later In

Costa Rica...

The scenery in Costa Rica completely amazing. White sandy beaches, the bluest water I've ever seen. Serene waterfalls, and the people were super friendly.

"This is complete paradise, Kevin! I really needed this trip. Thank you so much for bringing us here."

"No problem. We needed to get away." He said as we walked along the beach. I couldn't stop taking pictures of the scenery. Everything from the food, the waterfalls, the people. This was pretty amazing. It actually helped take my mind off of the miscarriage.

"I really want this moment to be special. We've been together for a while and nothing can replace the way that I feel about you. I want to know if you will marry me again Crystal."

"What? Marry you? We're already married, Kevin." I said puzzled and sipping a Mai Tai drink, as we lay along the sandy beach watching the waters cascade.

"Let's renew our vows. This time, let's have a big wedding at a church. I'm serious. When we get back to the states that's what we'll do to celebrate our many years together. Think of it as a rebirth. For us to let the old things die and get ready for a new future."

"Yes, I'd love to do that! I can't wait."

Kevin was so sweet. Paying for this expensive trip. Now we were renewing our vows. This time having an elaborate wedding. I couldn't wait to walk down the aisle in my white gown and see him standing at the end of the altar looking at me with love in his eyes. I just hoped all this bliss that I was truly feeling would last. But as everyone knows, nothing last forever and if things are too good to be true hell, they usually are. I couldn't take any more pain from Kevin. So, I prayed that this time he would be coming correct. Only time would tell.

Chapter 16
Things Unsaid / Trish

If Kevin thought, he could run from me and this baby he had another thing coming. Damn, I was tired of pretending. The truth needed to be brought to the light. Trish Yearwood refused to be a single mother. I had everything I wanted. All I needed to do was get rid of Crystal. That bitch was like a thorn in my side.

After my prenatal appointment, Kevin drove me home.

"Look Kevin, this baby is coming whether you want it to or not. I don't know how much longer you want to keep this secret from your wife. But personally, I don't give a damn about how she feels. We have everything we need except that bitch—"

"Trish, I will take care of the baby just to stay off of child support but my love for Crystal hasn't changed at all. She's really been going through a lot and I need to be there for her." He said.

"Are you serious? You need to be there for her? I'm the one that's pregnant with your child. I think your loyalty lies with me."

"Trish! Crystal is my wife! What part of that don't you understand? I have a wife and a marriage."

"But I didn't have sex and create this fucking baby all on my own Kevin. Maybe you should have told your damn dick that you were married."

"Whatever, Trish. Nothing has changed. You need to get that shit through your dense head. I'm here for the baby not you. I love Crystal and she will forever be my wife. I'm just trying to keep my wife from finding out the truth. Do you understand how hard it is living two separate lives?"

"You wouldn't have to live that way if you'd just leave her for me like I told you to do years ago. You're so hard-headed, Kevin. You know that I am the one who truly makes you happy. I'm having your baby. I'm giving you everything you've always wanted. Stop pretending that you love her. It's me Trish. How long have we been doing this?" I asked him while leaning over to give him a passionate kiss on the lips.

As I begin to kiss him, I felt him caressing my inner thigh. This baby would be the key that changed things around for us. Come on, what man isn't going to be there for a woman carrying his child. His son. Yes, I'm giving him his first- born child- a son. Something that Crystal couldn't do.

Two

Months

Later...

Chapter 17

Wedding Bell Blues - The Truth Comes Out

Today, was one of the most amazing days of my life! Renewing my vows with my husband Kevin Rose. I again, would be Crystal Rose. Me and my husband had shared many wonderful years together. We didn't have the finances all those years ago for a huge elaborate wedding and I couldn't wait to walk down the aisle towards my king.

Sitting in the dressing room of the church while my bridesmaids all did my hair and makeup. I saw everyone except my maid of honor, Trish Yearwood. We'd been friends since childhood. She was my ride or die. We've done everything together, even college. I work as an anchor for a prestigious news channel. While she works as a reporter. Lost in my mental trance, I had a friend tap me on the shoulder.

"How does it look, Crystal?" My bridesmaid, Amanda questioned.

"It looks great! You always do great work when I need it."

"Okay, where is everybody? Where is Trish? Anyway, let's go. It's time!"

"Oh, no! I'm not ready!" I squealed.

"Too late!"

I grabbed my bouquet and my friend placed my veil over my face. We walked towards the chapel. Instantly, I felt butterflies in my stomach.

"Sister Rose, we have a slight problem. We haven't been able to find Brother Rose, nor Sister Yearwood," The pastor said, panicking.

Oh no! I thought.

I stormed into the chapel and searched everywhere for my husband. I know he would show up. We had planned for months now. I looked all around and still couldn't find neither one of them. I didn't know what was going on.

My friends approached me saying they finally found them. I followed my bridesmaids and walked toward where they were leading me to let my husband know that it was time to get the ceremony started. Instead, I get the biggest shock of my life.

The doors of the storage closet I was told they were in flew open. My so-called husband was screwing my best friend against the wall of a freaking church in a closet. Everyone was appalled at this sight. I was truly disgusted.

They were going at it until I walked up toward them. All of his groomsmen and my bridesmaids were standing around. They gathered themselves together and my husband just stared at me.

I walked right up to him and slapped the piss out of him. I was in a church so I refused to curse right now. Trish walked right out of the room and began down the hall. I walked up toward her and grabbed her arm.

"How the heck could you do this to me? This is my husband! What is wrong with you, Trish?"

"What?"

"What do you mean, 'what'? You just screwed my husband! My husband! You can't get your own man!"

"Your man? You're so silly. You mean, 'our' man. You remember when I told you I was pregnant. Guess, who the father is!" she declared, rubbing her protruding belly. "I've been trying to ruin your' life since college. It's just now that you're finally catching on," she taunted.

I know I was in the house of the Lord, but I just couldn't take it anymore.

"You bitch!"

I jumped on Trish and we began fighting. Yes, we were scrapping inside of a church. Everyone rushed over to break us up. I remember Amanda pulling me off Trish and holding me back. Full of adrenaline, I wanted to kick both their asses.

I saw him standing against the wall. He looked so pathetic. I pulled my ring off my finger and threw it at him.

"It's over! Give me a divorce. Go be with that ho!" I yelled before me and my bridesmaids walked out of the chapel.

I knew Trish was a snake, but I tried to deny it. I tried to overlook it for years. Seeing the things she did with other friends and even her sister. I just never thought she'd be the one to stab me in the back. It was plain to see that this bitch had it out for me.

Amanda tried to convince me to follow her to the car, but I had unfinished business to attend to. I ran up to Trish and punched her in the face until she fell to the ground. I didn't really care that we were in the church parking lot. This bitch deserved everything she got.

"Crystal! Crystal, stop! You're going to kill her, stop!"

There was so much adrenaline coursing through my veins that I didn't care that I'd given that bitch a black eye and a bloody nose. Hell, I even forgot she was pregnant. *Wait, she is pregnant.* That is what made me stop from killing this bitch. I backed away and turned my frustration to Kevin, who was standing against the building looking pitiful. I ran up to him and smacked the hell out of him again.

"How could you get another woman pregnant? I was pregnant with our baby, then I lost it. I lost our baby. I miscarried our baby! But you turn around and get this trick pregnant! You took life from me and give it away to this ho! I hate you! I fucking hate your ass, Kevin! I hate the fucking moment I ever met your ass. Get your shit and the get the fuck out of my life!"

Amanda pulled me away and carried me to the car. My wedding dress, that represented our wonderful years together now tarnished in pain, regret and sorrow. The heart that I felt for him, now torn and shattered to pieces. Our entire marriage was a complete and utter fucking lie! Amanda drove me over to her place because she knew if I saw Kevin back at our place, I'd probably kill him. He hid an entire pregnancy from me. He had a baby outside of our marriage. I lost the child that I tried to give to him but couldn't.

Amanda tried to calm me down but nothing she could possibly do took away the anger and frustration that raged within me. I wanted Trish dead. *That bitch!*

"She's always wanted to destroy my life. Hell, she took the life I had with Kevin. But now she can have Kevin because, Child, I am through! Those low-life hoes can have each other!" I said to Amanda.

Chapter 18
The Aftermath

"I can't believe this. I can't believe this. It's been two weeks since I found out about this mess. But I still can't believe Kevin did all of this to me." I screamed out.

"I'm so sorry, Crystal. I really, truly am. But I understand how angry you are, which is why I have hidden all of the knives," Amanda joked.

"I'm not going to kill anyone, Amanda."

"I know. I'm just trying to make you laugh."

"I'm certainly not in a laughing mood."

"I know, and I'm sorry. But honestly, Kevin is a jerk for doing that to you."

"Did you know about any of this?" I asked.

"No, I did not. I would have told you if I knew something. But I've always told you Trish was a snake. You remember how fake she was in college. Trish is one of those people that if she's miserable, she wants you to be as well. Look, I have to take off and head to the office. I wish you well. Look at it this way, pretty soon you'll be able to leave all of this behind."

"Yeah, you're right, Amanda."

Amanda gave me a nice hug and a look of sympathy as she headed out of the door. I began packing my suitcase to prepare for my relocation; I heard Kevin coming into the house. A sudden shock of anxiety filled my chest. This was the first time I'd seen him since everything hit the fan. I couldn't believe he had the nerve to show his face to me again.

"Hey...hey...Crystal," he said, trying to make conversation.

I simply ignored him and continued packing. He walked up to me and touched my arm.

"Crystal! Look at me!"

"What? What is it? I don't have anything to say to your lying, cheating ass."

Walking over to the end table, I grabbed a manila envelope and took out a few sheets of paper while handing them over to him.

"What's this? Divorce papers? Naw, come on Crystal. I won't let it end like this. I love you, Crystal."

"Oh, save it, Kevin! You don't mean that at all!"

"Crystal, I'm so sorry."

"You are right. You are so sorry! A sorry ass piece of shit. I can't believe I wasted so much time with you. I tried to give you everything you could ask for. But you decide to sleep with my best friend. Hell, that bitch isn't even a friend. You betrayed me, you lied. You slept with another woman and had a child outside of our marriage. You made your bed so why don't you lie in it."

"I'm not signing those papers, Crystal. I'm not going to let you go, Baby. We can fix this—"

"Fix it. There is nothing to fix!" I snapped at him.

"Yes, there is, Baby. I promise you, Honey. I ca-can change. She didn't mean anything to me. I love you."

I rolled my eyes, walked over to him and slapped the taste out of his mouth just for saying that garbage.

"I guess it hasn't occurred to you why I'm packing this suitcase. I am moving to Los Angeles. I'm going to be the lead morning anchor at KTLA. I've moved on, there's someone waiting for me. He's also an anchor. Sign the divorce papers so I can forget you ever existed."

"No. No. Fuck no. I will never let you go. Baby, you mean so much to me."

He came up to me and hugged me aggressively. I thought my arms would break. Kevin was a complete joke. Now that I knew what was going on and I was ready to leave, he wants to be such a devoted husband. *Too late for that, Bro. I'm doing much better without you. I'm going to be making six figures as a lead morning news anchor in a top five market. Even snagged me a new guy who will be my co-anchor. Crystal Hall is ready to finally drop Atlanta like a hot potato and move toward sunny skies and warm weather.*

"Let me go, Kevin. Kevin. Let me go! You weren't thinking about me nor this marriage when you slept with Trish. Now that you have gotten caught you want to sing the tune of sorry. No, you're only sorry because you got caught. Your apologies aren't worth any weight in my eyes. I loved you. I truly and honestly did. I was willing to overlook some of the deceitful things you've done behind my back. Trust I was never as naïve as I appeared to be. Now I want out of this marriage. No need for this to turn into an acrimonious divorce. Just sign the papers so we both can be free. Hope you enjoy your new life and baby with Trish Yearwood. If you'll excuse me, I'm going to grab my suitcase and head out. I'll be back for the rest of my things later. Goodbye Kevin."

I exited the home I spent years with Kevin Rose in, building and growing our marriage. This is how he repaid me. Sleeping with another woman and getting her pregnant. Not just any woman either. My damn best friend! I had my own choice words for her but that'd have to wait until I saw her repugnant ass at work. For now, I had a few loose ends I had to tie up at the station before I was able to leave for LALA land. Lord knows, I needed a fresh start and the best is yet to come.

Chapter 19
Oh, Baby! / Kevin & Trish

Pacing around the house, I could have slapped myself for letting Crystal get away. Crystal will always be the love of my life. She was the one. How did I let her walk out of my life? Why did I even sleep with Trish? Man, if I could turn back the hands of time I most certainly would. I curse the day I ever decided to sleep with her slutty ho-ass.

Breaking my thoughts, I heard a loud pounding at my door. I rushed to open it thinking it may be Crystal. Perhaps, having a change of mind. Unfortunately, I opened it and saw Trish's homewrecking ass, heavily pregnant standing in front of me standing on my porch.

"What the hell do you want? You already ruined my marriage. What the hell else do you want?"

"Um, what do you think?" she questioned with attitude pointing to her protruding belly.

"That's not my problem. That's yours." I said as I turned to shut the door in her face.

She blocks it with her arm. "You can't just shut me out Kevin. You created this situation. You need to be responsible for your, oh, I mean, 'our' child."

"I don't want this fucking child. I told you that shit a while ago. I told you to abort it. You didn't. Now you're stuck. Fix your own damn problem."

"This baby is coming soon. You need to stay with me."

"Stay with you? I'm not leaving my wife to be with you! How many damn times do I need to tell you so that I make it clear to you Trish, damn! Now get the fuck off of my porch before I call the cops!"

"Fuck you, Kevin. I'll just make you pay child support. Trifling ass son, of a bitch!"

"Whatever, not my fault. You got yourself into this."

"Not your fault! It takes two to make a baby! We'd been having sex together since college. Now you have the audacity to try and make it appear as if I did this shit to myself. Because now you've been caught? Brother, please. You fucked up. Tell your penis since it won't register to your damn brain." Trish said, walking away back to her car.

I slammed the door shut and could truly kick myself. *Is this really what my life has boiled down to?* Honestly, in a split-second, things can change. I was a married man with a beautiful wife that would give me the world. Now, I was on the verge of a divorce and having a baby by a woman I didn't even like. Fellas, let this be a lesson to you. Think with your first brain and not your little brain. It may just cost you the love of your life, your freedom, hell, even your sanity.

Going back into the house, I tried to get the thought out of my head. But as much as I hated Trish, I had to admit that she was right. I had an obligation to the child I created, whether I wanted it or not. My son was coming and he was coming fast. Trish was nine months pregnant. Due any day. It might not have been the way I wanted it, but this little man was still my family. That was my son. He was my son.

The next week while working, I got continuous buzzes on my phone. I took my first break and checked my voicemails. Shockingly enough, there were quite a few from Trish, she was in labor. My son had made his appearance in the world. I truly had mixed emotions about the situation. As a man, this moment brought out another side of me. But as a husband who is trying his best to learn from his mistakes and hold on to the best thing that ever happened to him, I couldn't have been more pissed. I ran up to my boss and explained the situation. Luckily, he allowed me to leave early for the rest of the day and I headed down to the hospital to see my brand-new son. Jacob Ross Yearwood. A beautiful baby boy with a head full of hair.

"Aren't you going to come over here and hold your son?" Trish questioned me with an attitude.

"Look, I don't even know if this really is my son. Perhaps we should get a DNA test."

"Don't start that crap with me today. I've been through too much and I am certainly not in the mood. This is your son and you have to deal with it."

Honestly, the little man looked just like me. Really couldn't deny him if I wanted to. *Just ugh! Why did I mess with Trish of all people? I'll probably never get Crystal back now. What the hell was I thinking?* Is the question I ask myself everyday by getting myself in this fucked up ass situation.

A
Couple of
Months
Later...

Chapter 20
Jealously Runs Deep / Crystal

"Didn't expect to find you here. Honestly, what are you doing here? We made things perfectly clear last month with those divorce proceedings. I'm just waiting on the finalization," I said to my pitiful ass husband oh, excuse me, ex-husband, as he stood on the doorstep to the house we once shared.

"I just wanted to talk to you Crystal. We can't even talk anymore?"

"Kevin, you have some nerve wanting to come down here to converse with me now. Where was all your willingness to talk with me while you were screwing my use to be best friend? Oh, now you have all the time in the world to talk and want to fix our marriage. I have a busy day today, now will you please leave."

"Come on, Crys, isn't our love worth that? We've been through too much to throw it all away."

Besties

"If you don't want your feelings hurt you might want to leave now before I slam the door in your face!" He was just not getting the hint.

"Look!" he excitedly grabbed the door to prevent me from closing it. "Why are you being so difficult? Don't you think there is something left salvaging here? How can you give up on us so fast?"

I gestured for him to come inside because the next choice of words for him were not going to be pretty and I certainly didn't want my neighbors to hear us yelling at one another.

"You can't be serious right now, Kevin!"

"You aren't?"

I began pacing around the living room, breathing hard. Everything in me wanted to kick his narrow ass. Because he must have forgotten what led to our divorce in the first place. If he had so much to say and so much love, where the hell was it all those years? I loved Kevin since day one and he did nothing but lie to me the entire time.

"Dammit, Kevin! You have a baby with another woman! You messed up this marriage. Not me. That was all you. What more do you want from me? I am just trying to get past this mess and move on with my life. Go be with Trish since you wanted her so badly. Kevin, you created an entire family behind my back. Yet, you don't think I should be upset? Just think if I'd done the same thing to you. Trust me, you would be pissed. So, just let it go. I am done. I'm done, Kevin."

Kevin walked over to me and tried to hug me. I blocked him. I didn't want that cheater touching me at all.

"I'm not going to give you up, Crystal. I don't care about the divorce. I'm not letting you go. You not leaving me."

"Kevin, you sound psycho, please leave. Leave, Kevin. Before I call the cops."

He was beginning to get a little too weird for me.

"I'm never letting you go, Crystal. I love you, girl. You know I'll never find anyone as special as you," he said to me repeatedly as he threw his hands around me, unwanted. I pushed him away from me and he slightly stumbled over himself.

"Are you drunk?" I questioned.

"So, what if I am? Living without you has drove me to drink."

"Kevin, I have to get to work and we aren't getting anywhere. Will you please leave, damn!"

"Fine, I got stuff I have to do as well. But best believe, I will never let you go. You are mine forever Crystal," he stated to me as he finally made his exit.

I threw up my hands in utter disgust, grabbed my belongings and headed to work a little shortly after.

The time had finally come. My contract with the Atlanta news station had ended. This was the last day at FOX5 and I would now be free to start at FOX11 in Los Angeles. Timing couldn't have been any better. I pulled up to the station and let out a long sigh. I'd worked so hard to get to where I was and now this was my very last time signing on as an anchor in my hometown. Good times, many good times I had with the staff of Fox5 Atlanta. I walked through the door and signed my name in the guest book as I always do and then proceed over to the break room. As I walked in, I received a huge, "Surprise!" from all my co-workers.

They really dressed it up in my favorite colors of crimson and cream. Of course, my soror colors. The table that sat in the middle of the room even showed a display of gifts, party favors as well as greeting cards they purchased for me. My co-workers really went all out for me.

"What is the meaning of all this?" I asked.

"It's your going away party! We're so proud of you. You're going to be awesome in Los Angeles. Congrats Crystal!" Rachel, one of the morning producers stated.

"Awe, thanks so much guys! I appreciate this so much."

Now I really felt bad about leaving my Atlanta friends. I looked around the room and saw everyone so elated for me. All but Trish, who appeared to be a looking a bit smug. I honestly, couldn't believe this bitch still worked here. It took every ounce of strength not to whoop her skank ass every chance I saw her.

Trish approached me with her arms stretched out to give me a hug.

"You know, I just had to come over and say I'm sorry for everything that has happened between us. Please know that I never meant to hurt you. I don't know what I was thinking, you've always been such a good friend. Congrats on your new job," she said as she walked over to me. "You might want to watch your back or you might not make it to L.A. If you know what I mean," she whispered in my ear and then walked off.

"Um, excuse me, is that a threat?" I shot back at her.

She just cut her eyes at me and continued walking out of the break room.

Our news producer came over to us and started talking about today's broadcast which we needed to get started in about fifteen minutes.

"Hey everybody. Just had to say, thanks to our good buddy, Tim. He was the one who put all this together for you, Crystal. We all just pitched in. Congrats again, Crystal. We're very sad to let you go. I remember when you started as an intern. You have certainly worked your way up. I know you're going to be great! Now, let's get ready to work."

I giggled to myself as my co-workers applauded for me. Before scattering over to the newsroom, I made a quick dash to the restroom to phone Amanda; something just didn't sit right with me.

"Hey, Amanda you there? Alright, listen, I don't have a lot of time. But just watch out for me today. This chick Trish said some funny stuff to me. You know I'm afraid of no one, but something just doesn't feel right with me. Yeah, thanks, just watch my back. Can't trust this girl. Look, I got to go but I'll hit you up again soon."

Later that day, I made my last appearance with Atlanta news. This was a very sad day but after everything I'd been through, it was certainly time to move on.

"Alright, Atlanta. We've got some bittersweet news for you all. This is my last day doing this newscast. I will be moving on to our sister station over in Los Angeles FOX11 doing the morning newscast. I hate to leave you guys! But I am officially signing off tonight. Be great guys!" I said as I finally signed off for the last time.

I took off my mic and proceeded to grab my belongings from my news desk to make room for my replacement that's coming in tomorrow. The time read a little past midnight on my iPhone X1 as I hopped into my vehicle to head home. Driving along on the freeway, I spotted a car behind me with bright lights on following behind me a little bit too quickly. I thought nothing more of it until I got rear ended and almost collided into a pole near the offramp. I pulled over to the side as the person behind me swerved and drove off.

I couldn't believe what just happened. I was in shock and gasping for breath with my hand over my chest. Luckily, the impact wasn't enough to cause any harm or damage. Pulling myself together, I finally got back on the road and headed home. But just when I thought things were over and I was trying to settle within my home, there was a loud shatter of glass coming from my living room. Coming from the kitchen to grab a bite to eat, I grabbed a butcher knife as I saw an anonymous figure walking toward me.

"Crystal, Crystal, Crystal. You little self-centered bitch. Everything just has to be about you huh?" the voice sounded familiar.

"Trish! What the fuck are you doing here?"

She began to charge at me and we tussled around for the knife as it was pressed tightly within my hand. As much as I tried to hold on, I couldn't. She knocked it out of my hand when I fell to the floor. Trish overpowered me; she was pure crazy. Her eyes had a look of rage within them. She stabbed me in the side of my stomach. I let out wails of agony and pain.

"Now I finally have a chance to do what I should have done since day one; end your life bitch!" She yelled as she attempted to stab me again.

Trish pulled me by my hair and started punching me in the face.

"What is your problem? You already had the baby. You got to give him what I couldn't. What's wrong with you?" I questioned as I tried to fight back blocking my face.

"Shut up! You always had to have the perfect fucking life. I always hated you, little conceited as bitch!" She drew her hand back to stab me again but before she had a chance to, I heard three gunshots going off and then Trish fell to the floor. Immediately, I scooted over so her body wouldn't fall over on me. The only thing I could think of is how the hell did she get shot. Then I looked up and see Amanda running over to me with a gun in her hand. She bandaged my wounds with some nearby cloth that was lying over my couch, then called the police.

"I can't believe this crazy bitch tried to kill you."

"I'm just glad you came when you did. I would have died without you."

"You told me to watch your back. I'm just sorry I didn't come sooner."

Eventually, the police did come, and Amanda explained everything to the officers. The EMS came and rushed me to the hospital. Thankfully, the wounds were not fatal and nothing that would impact my physical health. I stayed in the hospital for a couple days before I was released.

A week later, after my full recovery and just being able to process everything that happened, I convinced Amanda to get on a plane with me to Los Angeles. After everything I'd been through, I finally understood the true definition of friendship.

Excerpt

From

An

Upcoming

Novel...

"Leilani's Secret"

I was coming home from another long night of rehearsal of, Fighting Back, the current Hollywood movie that I was working on. The rain and thunderstorm had gotten worse as I turned to pull up the driveway. Luckily, I had my umbrella lying in the back seat. I checked to see what time it was, and my digital clock read to me: 1:15 am. I could not believe that the time had flown past like that. I hoped Leon was still sleeping so I could sneak into the house unnoticed.

I turned off the ignition to my Porsche, grabbed my umbrella and walked toward the porch. I fumbled through my purse to find my house keys. I finally unlocked the door and stepped into the house. Looking around, a bit startled, it was darker inside the house than outside. I tried to reach for a light switch and the next thing I knew, I heard Leon's voice pounding from the end of the hallway as I saw a tall figure running toward me. I slid against the wall as I anticipated what would happen next.

"What the hell are you doing coming home so fucking late, Leilani?" he asked, yelling at me.

"Leon, you knew I had rehearsal tonight. I just did not expect it to last so long. Sorry, I lost track of time. But it is not the first time, so why are you always trippin'?" I stated as I tried to plead my case.

"That's just it, shit! I'm tired of you coming home so fucking late all the damn time. What the fuck are you doing that you have to keep coming home so late? Are you cheating on me? You're cheating, aren't you?"

"No, Leon. I am not cheating on you. I don't have time to cheat any damn way."

"What? So, you are saying if you had the time you would?"

"Leon, you're taking it the wrong way, you know what I mean. I'm tired; I don't have time for this. I just want to go to sleep."

"Hell no, fuck that! I'm not letting you get away from me that easily. I'll be damned if you cheat on me and think you can get away with it!" he repeated over and over.

"I'm not cheating on you! What the hell is wrong with you? I was at work! Why do you always think someone is cheating on you? Are you cheating on me? Do you feel guilty for some stupid shit that you did? Now you just want to blame that shit on me? I'm tired of this, Leon. Damn."

"I don't know who the fuck you think you're talking to like that!" he said as the thunder clapped and the rain poured down harder.

It was one thing to be arguing but I do not think the weather helped the situation. The more the thunder boomed, the scarier it made Leon's voice appear to be. I just wanted this night to be over. But it was far from being done.

I walked past him toward the stairs; I didn't want to argue with him tonight. He knew I'd never cheat on him, so I didn't know where all this was coming from. I just wanted to crawl into bed and get a good night's sleep. Well, a good morning's sleep. But he just wouldn't let this go.

"No! I'm not letting you walk away from this shit!" he said, as he pulled me from my waist and threw me onto the floor.

I tried to rise to my feet, but he started to punch me in the face. I blocked my face with my hands and kicked him in the groin. I tried to run to the den as fast as I could to escape from Leon's treacherous fit. *Here we go again*, I thought. I couldn't take coming home to his abusive ways. I did not need this. I sure as hell did not deserve this. Every night we fought. Every night we argue, every night I'd end up bloodied and bruised. Every night he'd lie as he looked me in my eyes and told me that he loved me. Every night I'd cry as I felt that each day another part of me died.

"You bitch! Wait to I get my hands on you. I'm going to kick your ass!"

"Leon! Leon, just please leave me alone! I'm tired of going through this with you. You're going fucking insane!"

"Oh, I'm the one that's insane while you're going out doing God know what with God know who."

I sat in the den with the door locked wondering why I continued to endure this pain and misery from a man that clearly didn't love me. I knew that I deserved better, but I was just too damn afraid to leave him. I was paralyzed in fear and stuck in a loveless relationship. The house turned quiet and even the thunder stopped roaring. I assumed that Leon had given up his pursuit of trying to chase me down. I slowly crept to the door, still everything seemed silent. I opened the door and walked into the hallway. I proceeded down the hall toward the downstairs bedroom. Sadly, the next thing I knew, Leon had appeared out of nowhere.

"You thought I would forget about this shit!" he shouted.

As soon as I heard his voice, I stood frozen in fear; that paralyzing feeling came over my body again. I don't know what happened next because moments later, I felt Leon hit me in the back of the head with a metal baseball bat. I fell to the floor. I blacked out. I know I could've died that night. All this shit this man has put me through. I couldn't take it anymore, so why the fuck was I doing it? This was just the tip of the iceberg.

Maybe I should back up a minute and explain how everything got so rough between me and Leon. Because honestly speaking, things were not always this horrific between us. Let me tell you the story of how Leon and I first started dating. One meeting changed my entire life as

I struggled to juggle college and my professional acting career. I guess love really can be deadly.

www.ingramcontent.com/pod-product-compliance
Lightning Source LLC
Chambersburg PA
CBHW021117130626
46554CB00002B/731